Dealing with

DISAPPOINTMENT

Learning how to CARRY ON

Jasmine Brooke

FOX EYE
PUBLISHING

Antelope always had very high **HOPES**. She always believed that everything would **GO HER WAY**.

She thought she could win every prize.

She thought she could do everything.

But because Antelope **EXPECTED** everything to go her way, it could lead to **DISAPPOINTMENT**.

3

At school, it was time for the story competition. Mrs Tree told everyone, "We will read all the stories aloud and then vote for the one we like the best."

Antelope was **SURE** she would win. She had high **HOPES** that it would surely go her way.

When everyone had finished writing, they read the stories one by one. It was then time to vote, Antelope was so excited!

She was **SURE** she would hear her name. "And the winner is ..." called Mrs Tree. Antelope gasped. Bear's story had won!

DISAPPOINTED, Antelope had been so **SURE** she would win. "It isn't fair," she sighed. "Why didn't it go my way?"

In the afternoon, Mrs Tree asked everyone to paint a picture. "We will show them at the end of the day," she told the class, "and vote for the one we like the best."

Everyone was excited and started to paint, all hoping they might win. But Antelope was a little too excited.

She was **SURE** she'd win. This time, Antelope felt it would surely go her way.

Everyone finished painting.
It was then time to vote!
Antelope was so excited,
she was **SURE** she would
be the winner. "And the winner
is ... Zebra!" called Mrs Tree.

Antelope was so
DISAPPOINTED.

She sighed, "Why didn't it go my way?"

11

When it was time to go home,
Peacock handed out invitations.
"It's my birthday party this
weekend," he told everyone.
"You are all invited!"

Antelope was very excited.
"I'm **SURE** I can come!" she
told Peacock. But then, she
remembered and sighed, "Oh
no, I can't go! I will be away."

Then poor Antelope sobbed,
"**NOTHING** is going my way!"

Mrs Tree had been watching. She knew Antelope had such high **HOPES**.

"Can I tell you a secret?" Mrs Tree asked. Antelope nodded, and sniffed. "I try to stay positive every day and if things go wrong, I **CARRY ON**. If I do win a prize or am invited to a party, it's a lovely surprise!"

Then Mrs Tree said,
"Now, let's see what next
week brings. I have very
high **HOPES** indeed!"

The next week, Antelope
enjoyed writing her story.
She knew even if she did
not win, she would carry on.

Soon it was time to vote. "The
winner is ..." smiled Mrs Tree.
Antelope gasped. She had won.
What a lovely surprise!

Antelope had learnt to manage her **HOPES**, and learnt to always carry on.

Words and feelings

Antelope was disappointed when things didn't go her way and found it hard to carry on.

DISAPPOINTMENT

HOPES

There are a lot of words to do with disappointment, hope and carrying on in this book. Can you remember them?

DISAPPOINTED

HOPE

CARRY ON

19

Let's talk about behaviour

This series helps children to understand and manage difficult emotions and behaviours. The animal characters in the series have been created to show human behaviour that is often seen in young children, and which they may find difficult to manage.

Dealing with Disappointment

The story in this book examines issues around hope, expectation and disappointment. It looks at how having overly high expectations can lead to disappointment.

   The book is designed to show young children how they can manage their behaviour, build resilience and carry on.

How to use this book

You can read this book with one child or a group of children. The book can be used to begin a discussion around complex behaviour such as learning to manage disappointment.

   The book is also a reading aid, with enlarged and repeated words to help children to develop their reading skills.

How to read the story

Before beginning the story, ensure that the children you are reading to are relaxed and focused.

Take time to look at the enlarged words and the illustrations, and discuss what this book might be about before reading the story.

New words can be tricky for young children to approach. Sounding them out first, slowly and repeatedly, can help children to learn the words and become familiar with them.

How to discuss the story

When you have finished reading the story, use these questions and discussion points to examine the theme of the story with children and explore the emotions and behaviours within it:

- What do you think the story was about? Have you been in a situation in which you were disappointed? What was that situation? For example, did you not win a prize that you hoped you would win? Encourage the children to talk about their experiences.
- Talk about ways that people can cope with disappointment and build resilience. For example, think about how you can focus on enjoying experiences and always keep in mind that if something doesn't go your way today, it may well do in the future. Talk to the children about what tools they think might work for them and why.
- Discuss what it is like to manage expectations. Explain that Antelope did not manage her expectations and believed everything would go her way, and that led to disappointment.
- Talk about why it is important to be resilient and how that can help children to manage different situations.

Titles in the series

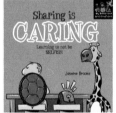

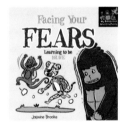

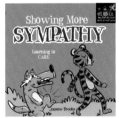

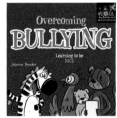

First published in 2023 by Fox Eye Publishing
Unit 31, Vulcan House Business Centre,
Vulcan Road, Leicester, LE5 3EF
www.foxeyepublishing.com

Author: Jasmine Brooke
Art director: Paul Phillips
Cover designer: Emma Bailey & Salma Thadha
Editor: Jenny Rush

All illustrations by Novel

ISBN 978-1-80445-297-4

A catalogue record for this book is available from the
British Library

Printed in China